TOUGH AS THEY CRUMB

RAISED AND GLAZED COZY MYSTERIES,
BOOK 26

EMMA AINSLEY

SUMMER PRESCOTT BOOKS PUBLISHING

CHAPTER ONE

"I think the crowd is just about right," Maggie Sharpe announced to her grumpiest employee. Orson Hawley stood just outside the window of her donut truck, an investment she had made after the success of her original donut shop located in her hometown of Dogwood Mountain, Missouri. Since inheriting the business and her small cottage home from her late great-aunt, Marjorie Getz, Maggie had seen the business grow into a second location.

The food truck brought the goodness of the donut shop to remote locations. This time, the location was just outside the small town, an area recently incorporated by the town's mayor, Jason Savino. Maggie took to running the food truck herself for the event. As an at-large member of the Dogwood

Mountain City Council, her best friend and business partner Ruby Cobb was on hand as an official member of the city's delegation to cut the ribbon on Dogwood Mountain West, the newly added section of town.

While Maggie ran the food truck, two of her other employees, Myra Sawyer Macklin and Naomi Gardner took care of business back at the brick and mortar store. Orson was along to make sure Maggie had her ducks in a row, as he so lovingly reminded her every five minutes. Brett Mission, her fiancé and the county sheriff, was on hand as well to appear in the photos for the local paper and to offer an air of security for the town's dignitaries.

On one of the trips Brett made to see her at the food truck, she whined to him about Orson and his doting. He was doing much more doting than working.

"I'm sure Orson would step up and help out in the event you become overwhelmed," Brett had said. "Until then, he's just being his regular old self and you love him for it."

Maggie figured he was right. Orson could be difficult, but he'd also been very helpful. Lately, he'd taken over most of the paperwork for the shop to reduce the hours on his feet. She was grateful he was still able to be up and about, even if much of that time was spent scowling at her for one reason or another.

"Do you need a refill on your coffee, Orson?" Maggie leaned out the order window and checked in on him.

"Yeah, but I'm going to brew it myself this time," he said, rising from his seat at the picnic table next to the truck. Maggie grinned and waited for him to make his way on board.

"Can you watch things for a second for me?" she asked when he was fully inside. "I want to run up front and see Ruby with the mayor and the rest of the city council when they cut the ribbon."

"Yeah, yeah," Orson said, waving his hand at her. "You go on and run about. Leave this old man to take care of things back here. You know I'll get things done while you're gone."

Most of the crowd had gathered around the small post office that would serve the annexed part of town. The city government would remain the same, but there would be some differences in terms of utilities and tax rates. The town of Dogwood Mountain had overwhelmingly passed a one percent sales tax hike to support the development and infrastructure of the annexed area.

Maggie had only learned about the plans to add

the area around the same time the rest of the public did. Later Ruby revealed the fact that the plan had been in the works for some time, but the council and the mayor had failed to see eye to eye on the addition until the sales tax plan had been conceived. With the additional tax, Dogwood Mountain West would essentially pay for its own development while the coffers of the entire city could be filled with the profits from any new businesses and development that would come along.

Ruby waved her hand slightly from her place on the temporary dais erected in front of the post office for the occasion. She sat at one end of the line of chairs placed for the mayor and the members of city council. She had joked with Maggie and the others earlier that the only reason a federal building like the post office had been selected for the ribbon cutting was because so far it was the only building in town that bore the name "Dogwood Mountain West."

"Told you Orson would step up and take over for you when you needed him to," Brett said from behind her. He brushed her waist with his hand, careful not to show too much affection in such a public setting, even though their recent engagement had been announced in several newspapers across the county.

"I know, but he made sure I knew he was doing

me a favor." Maggie chuckled. She slipped her hand into Brett's and squeezed slightly.

"Of course, he did." Brett grinned. "I swear the only thing that keeps that man young is the sass and vinegar in him."

"Vinegar is about right," Maggie said. While he had not said much about it, she suspected Brett held the opinion that she should ask Orson to stand in for her own father and walk her down the aisle at their wedding just as Myra had done. She'd considered it, just as she had considered asking her son Bradley to do the same. Thankfully, they still had time to figure it out. The wedding date had been set for late in the coming spring, after the youngest of Brett's three daughters graduated.

"Ladies and gentlemen," Mayor Savino announced into the microphone on the raised platform. "I think it's time we get this show on the road." A small cheer went up from the crowd. "There are a number of folks who deserve recognition for their contribution to this project."

Maggie zoned out a bit while the mayor launched into a two-minute long list of local businesses and individuals he wanted to thank for their work on the annexation. At last, he announced members of the city council and thanked them for the foresight to work alongside him to bring the project to life.

"Finally, let me say that with the incorporation of the Dogwood Mountain West area, we have entered into a new era of prosperity and economic growth. Soon we will be the destination for new businesses, new residents, and tourism in this part of the Ozarks. Thank you all for your attendance today and your constant support of our beautiful little town," the mayor continued. "Now, let's get to cutting that ribbon!"

Brett and Maggie applauded while the mayor wielded the ceremonial giant scissors and cut into the oversized ribbon. Once the ribbon was cut, cheers erupted from the crowd. Ruby joined the mayor and the other council members posing for photos for the local paper and the larger county newspaper while the other dignitaries milled about shaking hands and chatting with each other.

"Are you going to stick around and talk to Ruby?" Brett asked her.

Maggie shook her head. "I better get back and make sure Orson hasn't boxed the ears of some unsuspecting customer." She reached for his hand again and squeezed it before she turned to head back to the food truck.

"Ladies and gentlemen, one more thing," the mayor broke in suddenly on the mic. "I am completely remiss in forgetting to encourage you to head out and support the fine businesses that are represented here today. We have a small vendor fair going on down Cypress Street. Take a short walk and give some of these fine folks your business. Thank you."

"Well, that was nice," Brett whispered to her.

"Yeah, it actually was," Maggie said. She smiled as she walked back toward the very place the mayor had just encouraged the crowd to patronize.

CHAPTER TWO

Maggie checked over the donuts left in the display case and scanned the crowd. She had prepared for a light day, assuming the number of people in attendance for a civic matter would not reach the typical amount she could expect for another type of festival or event. But the crowd remained fairly steady.

Given the nature of the event, she had planned a simple menu, with one exception. Fall was one of her favorite times to introduce new donut flavors, even if the donut was only featured on a temporary basis. Maggie had scoured her cookbooks and the internet for a new idea, one she'd wanted to develop on her own and then present to the rest of the staff.

As a master chef, Ruby had the chops to bring in the most imaginative and exceptional flavors, and

Maggie never begrudged her that. But once in a while, it was nice to see the delight on her friend's face when she produced something unique on her own.

She had spent a week experimenting at home with a baked version of a gingerbread-flavored donut. Only Brett was the wiser, and her favorite taste tester. Maggie finally settled on a version of the baked donut with a maple glaze. The ginger flavor in the donut was offset by the addition of a rich molasses, but her favorite part was the simple glaze. She whipped together Greek yogurt, maple syrup, and coconut sugar until the ingredients dissolved into a perfect mixture to top the donut.

After her home experiments, Maggie brought her creation to Bradley and his staff in Hunter Springs and tested their reactions. When she was satisfied the donut was a hit, she surprised Ruby with a tray of donuts during their morning coffee break. Ruby had predicted another new fall classic flavor and suggested introducing the donut at the ribbon cutting ceremony. As usual, Ruby's instincts were dead on, and the gingerbread donuts had sold out first.

"Hey, Orson," she called out the window. "What do you think about running back to the store for a few more trays? I am almost out of everything here."

"Maybe we ought to shut down for the day," Orson grumbled. "How long do we really expect this crowd to continue, and to want breakfast?"

"Well, I'm not sure," Maggie admitted. "But they don't seem to be going anywhere, and I think most of the other vendors planned to be here until one this afternoon."

Orson groaned as he stood up from the picnic table. "I'm going to call the girls and see if they have any extras before I head over," he announced.

"Thanks," Maggie said. She failed to mention that she had already texted Naomi to check on the same thing.

While she waited for Orson to make his phone call, Maggie removed several trays from the display case and combined the remaining donuts onto a single tray. She quickly returned the trays to the sink filled with hot, soapy water and washed them for Orson to return to the donut shop.

Her back was turned to the windows while she washed up the trays. While she dried the final tray off with a clean towel, Maggie was suddenly aware of the rising volume of the crowd outside. She turned in time to see the backs of several crowd members. They were headed down the street toward the post office where the dais had been erected.

"Hurry up! There's a fight!" She heard a few members of the crowd speak over each other. Maggie moved to the order window and looked outside while she dried off her hands. "Orson!" she called. He stood in front of the truck watching as the crowd moved. "What's going on out there?"

"Don't know for sure," Orson said. "But I heard someone say there was some shouting from down the other way. I'm not sure who's doing the yelling, but it appears that these folks think it's a Saturday night boxing match or something."

"Let's hope not," Maggie said. She stepped outside the back door of the food truck and gazed toward the post office hoping to see something that would explain the sudden movement of the crowd into herd mode.

"I see Brooks and Brett," Orson said. He pointed toward the other end of the street. Maggie strained to see them but couldn't make them out in the crowd.

"If Brooks and Brett are headed that way, some-thing must be going on," she said. Not only was Brooks Macklin married to Myra, but he was also the town's chief of police and Brett's dear friend. She assumed he would be the one Brett would choose to stand up with him at their wedding as his best man.

"I still can't tell what's happening," Orson

complained. "Do you still want me to head over to the donut shop?"

"No," Maggie said with a sigh. "Let's see what happens here first. If the crowd is dispersed we won't have any reason to stick around anyway."

The din of voices from the other end of the street continued to rise while they stood talking. Maggie could see a growing number of people walking toward the post office. Word must have spread that there was some sort of incident going on.

"Too many darn looky-loos," Orson muttered. He threw his hands over his head and plopped back down at the picnic table.

"I think we're probably finished for the day," Maggie said a few moments later. She turned to open the door behind her. She might as well start the cleanup work for the truck. Maybe she could drive it back to the donut shop in time to steal away for a quick lunch with Brett.

As she opened the door, a shrill scream from the crowd had her spinning back around to see what was going on. From nearly two blocks away, she could see the crowd press in just to the right of where the dais was located in front of the post office. Most of the crowd had gone eerily quiet, until a man's voice cut through the hush. "Call 9-1-1," he shouted. "Somebody call an ambulance."

Maggie spotted the familiar uniforms of Brett and Brooks at last. She watched as they fought their way into the center of whatever was going on. Brooks pulled a few people out of his way as he went.

"Everyone, back up, now," he yelled at the top of his lungs. His voice was the deepest she had ever heard it.

A siren wailed close by. Maggie turned to see an ambulance between the houses on the next street over headed in the direction of the crowd as it raced toward the chaos.

"Orson," she hollered out to him. "Come inside the truck and help me get everything secured. I think we need to get ready to move on out of here."

"I think you're right," he said, quickly moving inside the food truck. He began closing and locking the large front windows. "You shut that display case and tend to the fridge and the cabinets."

"Good idea," Maggie said. "We can finish cleaning up back at the store."

Orson reached into the front pocket of his pants and pulled out a set of keys. "You go on and get my car and head back," he instructed. "I'll be along with the truck as soon as I can safely drive it out of here."

"Alright," Maggie said, taking the keys from him. "See you back there." Always the gallant protector, Maggie had learned years ago not to argue with Orson when he was in fatherly mode.

Maggie grabbed her purse and phone and walked down Cypress Street toward Orson's car. She went quickly, hoping nothing would escalate in the crowd behind her. When she reached his car, she unlocked the door with the key and settled into the front seat. As much as she loved Orson, she was not a fan of the thirty-year-old Oldsmobile he had recently purchased.

She glanced in the rear view mirror once to make sure the crowd was still occupied a few blocks away. Before she pulled the shifter into gear, she fired off a quick text to Brett letting him know she was headed back to the donut shop in Orson's car while he took over getting the food truck back. She sent a similar text to Ruby and then headed down the road.

Maggie put on her blinker at the next block and giggled at the loud "tick-tock, tick-tock" sound it made. She looked around the four-way intersection and spotted a dark green minivan parked in front of the stop sign to her right. She waited for the driver to pay attention to her, then beeped the horn lightly to get his or her attention. Dark tinting blocked her from seeing the driver clearly.

Without warning, the minivan roared across the intersection, turning left and barely missing the front of Orson's car. "Hey!" Maggie shouted and blared the horn at the vehicle. She sat stunned for a second, then remembering what was down the road from her, looked into the rear view mirror again to see where the van had gone. She breathed a deep sigh of relief when it was clear that the van had turned and gone another way, and not into the throng of people gathered on the other street.

After a few more deep breaths, she eased the car across the intersection and headed for the donut shop. Two blocks down, she glanced in her side mirror and noticed a woman dressed in a suit nearly running down the road behind her. Maggie pulled the car over and rolled down the window. She was unsure of the woman's name but by the way she was dressed, it appeared she was coming from the ribbon cutting.

"Hey, do you need a ride?" she called out the window. "I don't know what's going on back there, but I'm a friend and a business partner to Councilwoman Cobb. I own the donut shop here in town."

"I know who you are," the woman said. Her face was red and sweating under the large, white hair piled on top of her head. Despite the fact that it was late fall, the outside temperature was near 75 degrees.

"If you'd like a ride, I'm heading back to the donut shop," Maggie said.

"I'm just fine," she said. "There was an incident in the crowd, and I decided to walk home, thank you. I appreciate your offer, but please be on your way."

Maggie rolled up the window and pulled down the street. With the wave of her hand the woman had dismissed her. Between the incident with the green van and the rude woman, she was more than ready to lose herself in a sink full of dishes back at the donut shop. Maybe a little vigorous scrubbing of a few trays would take her mind off of the crowd, too.

Twenty minutes later, Orson pulled the food truck back through the parking lot and around to the back of the store. He parked it in the alley close to the back door and began carrying trays back inside.

"Did you hear any more about what was going on before you left?" she asked when she met him with his car keys.

"Not a word," Orson said. "Some idiot in a van came tearing past me at one point, but that was about all the excitement I was aware of."

Maggie nodded her head. "A dark green minivan," she said. "I met him at an intersection before I turned off of Cypress."

"I was waiting for him to plow right into the

crowd," Orson said. "Thank goodness he turned right at the last possible moment and went screeching out of there."

"I had the same concern," Maggie said.

Naomi joined them in the food truck a short time later. Together, they quickly had the truck clean and ready to return to its parking spot at the front of the store. Orson announced that he would move it back around front and climbed back into the driver's seat.

Almost as soon as he pulled the truck down the alley, Ruby pulled her pickup truck into her normal parking spot. She smoothed down the front of her pantsuit when she stepped down from the truck and headed inside. Her normally sun kissed face had paled. Her skin appeared clammy when she walked inside, nothing like the healthy glow she carried from running her own farm in addition to her work at the donut shop.

"You look like you've seen a ghost," Maggie said. She pulled out one of the wooden stools they often used in the back and ushered her best friend onto it. "What on earth happened out there?"

"Ruby? Are you alright?" Myra asked her. She headed toward her with a glass of ice water.

"Thank you," Ruby said at last. She tipped the

glass and drank down half of the water before she came up for breath.

"You're worrying me," Maggie said. "Say something."

Ruby nodded her head slowly. "I'm alright," she said. "Just a little shaken. The water helps."

"What happened?" Naomi repeated.

Ruby looked up. Her eyes were filled with tears. "I'm still not exactly sure," she said. "One minute we were all still gathered in small groups, shaking hands, and talking to people. The next thing I knew, the mayor let out a cry and fell down."

"He fell down?" Maggie asked. "Did he trip? Did someone push him?"

Ruby shook her head. "No, he fell forward with a pair of scissors sticking out of the back of him," she said. Her voice was thin and hollow. She looked at all three of the women gathered around her. "Mayor Savino is dead."

CHAPTER THREE

Maggie rushed forward to brace Ruby up on her stool. She swayed a little before her eyes rolled back in her head and then she slowly leaned forward. "Ruby? Are you okay?" Maggie shouted. She looked up at Myra. "Does she have any blood on her? Can you tell if she has been hurt?"

Myra stood back a couple of feet and scanned the back of Ruby's clothes. Naomi picked up one of her limp hands and began timing her pulse.

"Her heart is racing," Naomi announced. "I think she might be in some kind of shock."

"What should we do?" Myra asked.

"Nothing," Ruby said. Maggie felt as she stiffened a little and sat upright again. "I'm okay. I just feel a little woozy."

"I think you need to see a doctor," Maggie said.

"Fine," Ruby answered. "Drive me over to the urgent care." Maggie was shocked when she didn't argue with her or insist she was alright.

"I'll help you get her in the car," Myra announced. She flanked Ruby on the other side and wrapped her arm around her back as they walked outside to Maggie's car. Myra opened the passenger side door and helped ease her inside.

Orson burst through the back door and raced to the car. "I'm coming with you," he said and climbed into the back seat.

"I can get her into the clinic just fine," Maggie said. "You've already been through a lot today."

"Either you drive, or I will," he commanded. "Josie is on her way in to help the girls close the store down for the day. Zeke and Bradley said they would be over to help later if we need it."

"You called my son already?" Maggie asked. She turned the car on and headed down the alley.

"No, Naomi was on the phone with him when I came back through the kitchen," Orson said. "That's how I heard about what was going on."

Ruby leaned forward in the passenger seat. Her shoulders were hunched toward the dashboard, held back only by the seat belt. "Are you alright?" Maggie asked as she drove. She placed her hand on Ruby's arm and drew it up and down to rouse her. "Orson! She's not responding at all."

"Pull the car over," Orson shouted. Maggie eased quickly to the side of the road. "Get out and run over there to her. Pull her out and put her on the ground! Do it fast, Maggie!"

Maggie shoved her car into park and raced around to the passenger side. She pushed Ruby against the seat and reached in to unfasten the seat belt. As soon as the belt was free, Ruby's weight leaned against her.

"Come on out of there," she whispered, hooking her arms under Ruby's to pull her carefully onto the grass.

"She isn't conscious," Maggie shouted to Orson. He repeated the same words into the phone.

"Check her airway and make sure she isn't choking on something," he instructed.

Maggie pried Ruby's mouth open with her fingers and began feeling around for anything that might block her from breathing.

"I can't feel anything," she shouted. Tears streamed down her face.

"Is she breathing?" Orson shouted.

Maggie felt under Ruby's nose, then placed her ear on her chest. "I… I'm not sure," she cried.

She heard the slam of a door and looked up to see an older woman racing toward the side of the road from one of the houses on the block. "You have to start CPR," the woman shouted as she ran. She carried a small leather satchel with her. "Put your hands on her chest and pump three times."

She did as she was instructed. By the third pump, the woman skidded to her knees and moved Maggie's hands out of her way. She pressed hard into Ruby's chest, then paused to breathe into her mouth.

"I'm a nurse," the woman announced when she resumed the compressions. "Tell me about your friend, What happened? Do you know if she has any medical conditions?"

"I don't think she has any medical conditions," Maggie said quickly. "I don't know what happened. She is a member of the city council and was just at the ribbon cutting for the new section of town. She'd just gotten back to where we work, and she started acting like she was going to pass out or something."

"Okay," the nurse continued to pump Ruby's chest as she spoke. "Did one of you call an ambulance?"

"Yes. They're on their way," Orson said slowly.

Five minutes later, Maggie sat in the passenger seat of her own car while Orson drove. He followed the ambulance that carried Ruby to the hospital in Hunter Springs, the closest facility to their small town.

Her phone rang and she absentmindedly picked it up, not bothering to see who it was. She put Brett on speakerphone.

"Listen, Maggie. Three members of the city council are on their way to seek emergency medical treatment. Do you know where Ruby is? We think someone poisoned them."

She told him everything she knew and sat silently waiting for a reply.

"Oh, no. I'm so…"

"Who were they?" Maggie interrupted.

"Paul Simpson, Alice Reynolds, and Connor Tewes," Brett said.

"Connor is so young," Maggie said absently. "Are they as bad off as Ruby?"

"Not as bad from what you say about Ruby, though a couple of them are pretty ill," Brett said.

"Did they see anything? Do they know who did this?"

"No one saw a thing," he said. "We have nothing."

"I just don't understand how someone could have poisoned four members of the city council and stabbed the mayor with a pair of scissors, and nobody saw a thing," she said.

"I don't know what's going on just yet," Brett said. "But all you should worry about is Ruby getting better, okay?"

"Yeah," Maggie muttered. She hung up the phone and wiped the tears from her eyes.

"It's going to be alright," Orson said. His voice was firm. "I won't let it be anything else."

"I don't want this to be happening to anyone, but it's not fair that Ruby got whatever this is worse than everyone else."

He glanced over at Maggie. "Look, we both know something happened back there. It's no use pretending like there wasn't something else going on. I don't think this was an attack on Ruby."

"I know," Maggie said. She inhaled deeply and carefully, slowly letting her breath out. If she could keep her breathing under control, she could do the same with her emotions. "We have to remember that our mayor lost his life. Ruby is going to recover from whatever this is that she's dealing with."

Her phone rang again. This time, Bradley was calling her. A new wave of tears immediately overtook her.

"Mom, I just heard about what happened," he said. "Are you okay? Is everyone okay?"

"Your mom is fine, Bradley," Orson answered into the car's speakers for her. "But Ruby has been poisoned or something. We are driving behind the ambulance right now."

"Aunt Ruby? Is she okay?" Bradley asked.

"We're on our way to the hospital in Hunter Springs right now to find out," Maggie said when she recovered enough to speak. "She started acting funny when she got back from the ribbon cutting. Brett said that three more members of the city council fell ill as well."

"We're pulling into the hospital parking lot now, son," Orson said. "Your mom is alright, and we'll let you know as soon as we find out anything else about Ruby."

"Okay, Orson. Thank you," Bradley said. "I'm sending Zeke over in the morning to help run things. Can you let Naomi and Myra know? I figured they could use the help."

"I will," he said before he hung up the phone. Maggie nodded numbly to the news that Bradley's kitchen manager, Zeke Soren, would be around to take things over at the Dogwood Mountain location while she and her staff dealt with the concerns over Ruby's condition.

Orson followed the ambulance into the parking lot. When the ambulance driver failed to stop in front of the small emergency department, Maggie sat up higher in her seat. The ambulance continued to the far side of the parking lot.

"He's headed to the helicopter pad," Orson announced. Almost as soon as he could get the words out, Maggie heard the whip-whir of an incoming helicopter overhead.

"They're using an air ambulance," Maggie said. She felt small and powerless in her seat. "Why would they need to airlift her? They weren't even driving that fast on the way here."

"Listen to me, Maggie," Orson said. His voice was thick with emotion. He placed his hand firmly on her shoulder. "What has happened is that the paramedics in the ambulance have decided that her best option for treatment is going to be found at a larger hospital than this one. They are going to take her there the fastest way that they can. The hospital also has likely heard the same information we have about the other members of city council. Transferring her to another hospital could very well be a safety precaution."

Maggie nodded her head slowly. "I'm scared, Orson," she whispered. "I am afraid of losing my best friend."

"I am afraid, too," he said. "But we have to remember that this means she is going to the right place for the treatment she needs."

CHAPTER FOUR

Maggie leaned against the side of her car and watched as the helicopter took flight. Air whipped against her body, drying the tears that streamed down her face. When the helicopter was far enough away, she looked around for Orson and found him speaking to a member of the hospital staff. Maggie walked toward them.

"Yes, we are family, though not by blood," Orson insisted to the patient technician standing in front of him.

"I can't tell you where she is being taken," the younger woman said. "I'm sorry. Hospital policy."

"Let it go, Orson," Maggie said when he opened his mouth again to speak. "They have good reasons for the privacy policies."

They walked together back toward her car. She was inclined to let Orson drive back to Dogwood Mountain, but knew he was also struggling with his emotions. Without hesitation, he climbed in behind the wheel and started the car. Maggie buckled her seatbelt while he drove slowly toward the exit. She spotted the ambulance near the emergency department doors. One of the paramedics turned toward them and waved as they approached. Orson slowed to a stop and rolled down his window.

"We can't technically tell you where she has been taken," the paramedic said. He looked around as he spoke, then ducked his head closer to the window. "But I can tell you that she is being flown to a level one trauma center. We usually take patients to the closest one." With that, he patted the side of her car with his hand and stood up.

"Thank you," Maggie called after him. She picked up her phone and searched for the closest level one trauma center, finding it within a matter of seconds.

"Do you want to head there?" Orson asked her when he reached the edge of the parking lot.

"I want to go there right now and not leave again until I know if she is okay," Maggie said. "But I don't want to drag you all around everywhere. I don't know if spending hours in a hospital waiting room is something you can handle right now."

"Don't you worry about me," Orson said. "If you want to go, we'll go. If I need to head back home, I'll call for an Uber."

"You'll use an Uber?"

"Hey, I learned a thing or two in my old age," Orson said. He drove quickly through town and headed northwest on the highway toward Joplin. "Why don't you give Brett a quick call and let him know where you're going? Or at least send him a text. Same with your son. They're both going to be worried about you."

Maggie nodded and picked up her phone again. She typed out a short message to Brett and then to Bradley, before setting her phone in the console next to her.

"Are you doing okay?" Orson asked when they were about halfway to Joplin.

"I'm doing a little better," Maggie said. "I am scared to death for Ruby. I wish I knew what was going on, because not knowing is torture."

They said nothing more the rest of the journey to the hospital. Orson parked close to the front entrance under a light in the parking lot though it was still early in the day. They walked together into the hospital entrance and followed the directory to the intensive care waiting room, assuming that's where she'd been taken.

Maggie found a seat on the far end of the large room near the window. Orson hung around near the vending machines by the exits. While he made his selections, Maggie texted Brett that she had made it to the hospital with Orson.

"Any word on her condition?" Brett replied.

"We haven't seen anyone just yet," Maggie wrote back. "I planned to gather my thoughts and then I'll check in with the nurse's station."

"I'll text Bradley for you," Brett responded before ended their conversation. Maggie pushed her phone back inside her purse and smiled at Orson.

"I wasn't sure what sounded good to you," he said. His arms were filled with several snacks and two drinks for each of them. "Don't try to tell me that you aren't hungry because I know you haven't had anything since early this morning."

"I am starving," Maggie said. She selected a coke and a bottle of juice as well as a bag of trail mix.

"Thanks, Orson."

"You go on and take those brownies, too," he said. He pushed the brownies into her hand then sat back in his chair and twisted the top off of his coke.

"Brett said he would keep in touch with Bradley for me," Maggie said.

"That's nice of him," Orson said absently. He glanced toward the waiting room door. "I sure wish they would come out here and tell us something without us having to ask."

"Let's give it a minute and then we can check with the nurse's station," Maggie suggested.

Orson nodded his head. "They probably won't tell us anything anyway."

"They have to, don't they?" New tears filled Maggie's eyes. She had already forgotten about their exchange with the staff member at the hospital in Hunter Springs.

Orson slowly shook his head. "They really don't, sweetheart," he said. "But they might since we're really her only family." Maggie smiled a sad smile, but she already suspected that it would be an uphill battle to obtain much information.

"I wonder who she has down as her next of kin," Maggie said.

"Why do you wonder a thing like that?" Orson asked. "There's no reason to think she's going to need her next of kin."

"I don't mean because she, well, because she isn't going to make it," Maggie said. She swallowed the lump in her throat. "I only wonder if the next of kin is a friend and not a family member if they would be able to tell them something."

Orson shook his head. "They wouldn't put a non-relative as next of kin," he said. "Maybe as her I.C.E., but not as her kin."

"What do you mean?" Maggie asked. "Who would her ice be? What is an 'ice?'"

"In case of emergency," Orson said slowly. "It spells out the word 'ice.' I'm not sure who she would have listed, but mine is Myra. In case anything happens to me, Myra is my medical power of attorney, too."

Maggie was touched by the thought of Orson choosing someone with no legal or biological connection to be his medical decision maker.

"That's smart of you to pick someone close by," she said. "I guess Bradley is mine."

"That will change when you marry the sheriff," Orson teased. He winked at her to lighten the mood.

"I think I'm ready to ask," Maggie said. "I'm going over to the nurses' station to ask them what's going on."

"Right behind you," Orson said. He stood slowly and followed her across the waiting room. Maggie left her drink and her snacks on her seat; confident no one would bother her things while she took care of what she needed to.

The nurses' station was located just beyond the waiting room. It was stationed right outside of the double doors that led into the intensive care unit. "Excuse me," she said softly to the nurse behind the desk. His eyes were fixed on the screen in front of him. He was young, maybe a few years older than Bradley. She glanced at the tag on his scrubs. His name was Ryan, and he was a registered nurse.

"Can I help you?" Ryan asked. His eyes remained on the screen.

"Hi, my name is Maggie Sharpe, and my best friend was brought here by helicopter less than one hour ago," she began. "Is it possible to know how she is doing?"

"Are you a relative?"

"No, but I am her closest person, if you know what I mean," Maggie said. "Her name is Ruby Cobb. She is unmarried and has no children."

"Sorry, but I can't give you any information." He rubbed the scruffy whiskers on his chin and went back to his computer monitor.

"Please, sir," Maggie said. "I was with her when she started acting funny. I had to stop my car and drag her out of it and start CPR. Then this nurse came running out of her house and took over CPR. An ambulance took her to the little hospital in Hunter Springs and they met us all there with the life flight."

Ryan covered his mouse with his hand and looked up at her. "I'll tell you only one more time. I can't give you any information. Go have a seat and when someone gets here that we can talk to, have them come see us. Until then, there's no sense in standing here asking over and over."

"You've clearly forgotten how to speak with the public," a woman chimed in behind Ryan. Maggie stole a glance at her name tag. Her name was Tanesha and she, too, was an RN. When she caught a second glance at her tag, Maggie read the wording beneath her name said, "Trauma specialist."

"Now, folks, what was the name of the patient?"

"Tanesha, what about the privacy law?" Ryan whispered to her. If his aim was to be subtle, he had clearly missed the mark.

"It's not a violation if someone else is listed as her contact person. And there's only one way to find that out, which doesn't include being rude." She pulled a large computer tablet from the desk and tapped through the screen.

"Ruby Cobb," Maggie replied. "We drove here after the helicopter left Hunter Springs hospital."

"Do you have any identification with you?"

Maggie nodded and pulled her license from her purse. "Here," she said as she handed it over.

"You better be Ms. Sharpe, just like your identification says you are."

"I will swear to it," Maggie said, her heart racing.

"The good news is that we do have you on her records as her emergency contact," Tanesha said. "But she only lists one." She stared at Orson.

"Okay, I can take hints just fine," Orson said. He stepped back from the nurses' desk and returned to the waiting room.

CHAPTER FIVE

"Botulism?" Orson looked past her at the nurses' station she had just returned from. "How in the world could it have been botulism? Are we sure she wasn't just suffering from something emotional due to when she saw the mayor killed?"

Maggie shook her head. "They actually do suspect poisoning, Orson," she said. "Remember, three other members of the city council were also ill."

"And how do they look now?" Orson asked. "Because as far as I know, Ruby is the only person who had to be flown on a helicopter to a trauma hospital."

Maggie nodded and sat down next to him close to the exit. "She's not breathing very well on her own,

Orson. I think they are going to have to put her on a ventilator."

Orson shook his head. "I don't understand how it could have been botulism," Orson said. "When I was growing up, the threat of botulism was real, but it was usually from the food our mamas canned every summer."

"Botulism can come in different forms," Maggie said. "They think Ruby probably ingested or inhaled a great deal of it."

"Inhaled it?"

"Unfortunately," she said.

Orson shook his head but kept the rest of his thoughts to himself. Maggie returned to her previous seat and opened the brownies and popped a bite in her mouth. She opened the bottle of juice and took a long sip. "I need to increase my blood sugar," she said when Orson joined her again. "You were right about getting something to eat."

"Those brownies are good," he said. "I had some while you were in the other room with the nurse."

"I wish I could take some to Ruby." Maggie laughed softly. "She loves a good brownie."

Orson snapped his fingers. "We should develop a new brownie donut while she's in the hospital," he suggested. "We could surprise her when she returns to work. Because when she comes back, she is going to want something new to focus on."

Maggie reached for his hand and held it in her own. "You are exactly right, as usual," she said. "We absolutely need a new donut for her to focus on when she gets home."

They sat in silence for a little while longer. After six, Orson rose from his seat and announced that he needed to head back. He had a few medications of his own that he needed to take and was not prepared when he drove her to Joplin.

"Why don't you go on and take my car home," Maggie suggested. "That way you don't have to worry about waiting on a ride."

"How are you going to get home?" Orson asked.

"Brett or Bradley." Maggie smiled. "One of them will come and get me."

As if on cue, the waiting room door opened, and Brett walked in. "See? I told you." Maggie smiled. She rose from her chair and made it across the floor to him. He opened his arms and wrapped her up in a deep hug.

"I'll make sure she gets home safely," he said.

She closed her eyes and listened to his voice reverberate through his body. She felt comfort from the sound of his voice over her head.

"You sure she won't mind if I drive her car home?"

Maggie felt Brett shake his head slightly. "Just go on and drive her car home," he said quietly. His voice was almost a whisper. "We'll come by the house and pick it up."

Orson patted Maggie on her back before he walked out of the waiting room and headed home. Maggie held on to Brett for another half of a minute before she let him go. "Is there any news on who might have done this?" she asked when they walked together back to the chairs. "Because if there's a chance we figure out who was responsible, maybe they can find a better treatment."

"They do have treatments for botulism," Brett said.

Maggie sighed. "How are the other council members? Has anyone else been taken to the hospital?"

Brett nodded. "All of the others were hospitalized, although Ruby is the only one on a ventilator so far," he said.

Maggie felt her body sway a little. "So, they did go on and put her on it?" Maggie said.

"I'm afraid they had no choice," Brett said. "By the time she arrived here, her airway had collapsed."

"But the nurse told me they might need to, but that they hadn't," Maggie said.

"The nurse probably told you just enough so you'd have an idea what was going on, but nothing that would get you too upset until they had a better idea of what they're dealing with," Brett said.

"Oh, goodness," Maggie said, suddenly remembering the other major event of the day. "Did we hear right? Was the mayor killed?"

Brett nodded his head. "He was, and we have absolutely no suspects. Whoever did this was in and out fast, and so far no one has seen a thing."

"I wonder if the poisoning was a cover up," Maggie said, suddenly feeling a little more alert. "Maybe whoever did this only did it so they could distract everyone and reach the mayor."

"If that was their goal, their timing was way off," Brett said. "The council members started acting sick before the crowd began to gather around. It was because of that someone discovered that the mayor was doubled over."

Maggie sat quietly for a moment. She was grateful Orson had played mother hen with her and made her eat something. "I think whoever did this must not have been working alone. That would explain the bad timing. Working with someone else requires a lot of planning ahead of time. Everything has to be perfectly executed."

"Stop," Brett said quietly. "This is not a case you need any part of. You need to just focus on Ruby right now. Leave the crime fighting to the rest of us."

Maggie sighed. She pulled her phone out and silently began looking up news about the incident.

"You're going to try to figure out what happened anyway, aren't you?" he asked. "Of course you are. That's how you're going to get through this. Just promise me that you will be careful. Okay? We have no idea who did this or what they may have intended."

"What are you trying to say?"

"I'm saying that we have a murdered official and several other elected officials poisoned. "That could mean any number of things and I'd really rather you not be the one to find out what that thing is."

CHAPTER SIX

Maggie slept in the passenger seat of Brett's pickup truck while he drove them back to Dogwood Mountain. It was just past midnight when he took her keys from her and unlocked the door. She halfway stumbled into the living room and plopped down on the couch. "I'm just going to sleep here tonight," she said, leaning over.

"No, you're going to get up and go get ready for bed," Brett said. "I spoke with Bradley on the way home. Zeke is going to meet Naomi at the donut shop first thing in the morning and together they are going to open, but only until noon."

Brett pulled her up by her arms and guided her gently to her bedroom. She woke the following morning with a severe headache, a fuzzy sense of doom, and vague memories of how she got to bed in the first place.

Much to her surprise, she heard Brett snoring softly when she emerged from her bedroom. She headed into the kitchen and turned on the coffee pot.

"Maggie?" Brett called to her from the living room. "It's not even five in the morning."

"I have to get ready," she said.

Brett rose from the couch and sighed. He placed his arms around her shoulders and rocked her gently back and forth. "Sweetheart, when you went to bed last night, I told you that Zeke and Naomi are opening the donut shop today," he said. "You go on back to bed and get some more rest. I'll head into work myself around seven, okay? Let's get a little more sleep."

Maggie remembered their conversation and what Bradley had told her, when she switched the coffee pot back off and turned out the light above the sink. She padded back down the hall to her bedroom and pulled the covers back and climbed back into her bed. She closed her eyes and tried to settle back into sleep.

But her mind twisted over the images of Ruby as she was loaded from the ambulance into the helicopter. Her nostrils filled with the nearly odorless, nose-stinging smell of the hospital hallways. She could almost hear the beeps from the machines and the chatter from the nurses behind their desks. What she couldn't picture was Ruby smiling and joking around as she had done before the event in Dogwood Mountain West began the day before. She could see her waving slightly from her seat on the raised structure, but the sound of her best friend's laughter was absent from her mind.

Maggie felt the first hot tear flow slowly down her face. Soon both eyes filled with tears. She turned her face into her pillow when the sobs took over. For a solid fifteen minutes, Maggie cried her heart out for her friend and the very real possibility that she would never speak to her again. Fear and sadness crippled her while she lay there. She was powerless to do anything aside from letting the tears flow as the emotions washed over her.

She tried her best to stay quiet. Disturbing Brett in his sleep was the last thing she wanted to do. As part of the murder investigation, he had a difficult task ahead of him. The day before, Brooks himself had worked a fourteen-hour day, Brett told her. Providing security for the remaining members of the city government was paramount while the investigation into the incident continued. Maggie imagined Brett had a number of those long days in his future, too.

She did not want to deny him the chance to rest, but her motives were also selfish in nature. She planned to sit at the hospital until Ruby woke up. She wanted to be there when she opened her eyes again.

When she couldn't cry another tear, Maggie rolled over onto her back and stared at the ceiling over her bed. Most of the time, her room was still pitch black when she woke every morning. It was rare to see the early morning light dancing over her. She exhaled a long, deep sigh and sat up. She quickly gathered her clothes for the day and padded down the hall toward the bathroom. She could hear Brett's soft breathing in the living room.

She stood under the hot water and closed her eyes, willing her body to relax and release the tension in her muscles. Typically, Maggie showered at night after a long day around the heat and fryers in her donut shop kitchen. An early morning shower awakened her more than she expected.

When she opened her eyes, her mind began to turn around the idea that someone had attacked her best friend while she was out serving their community. The weight of the seriousness hit her once more. The mayor was dead. City council members had been poisoned.

"But, why?" she asked out loud. Who would have

wanted to kill the mayor? Aside from reading over the local paper several mornings each week, Maggie was not constantly aware of the happenings at City Hall. Ruby kept her informed on important things, but there was nothing that stood out as so dire it would lead to such an attack on the mayor and city council in a small southern Missouri town. True, such attacks on municipal governments had taken place before, but the circumstances were usually well documented in the news long before the attack happened.

What could have provoked such an attack on her small hometown? As far as she could tell, Brett had very little information to go on as well. She wondered if there was anyone who knew.

Maggie shut off the water and stepped out of the shower. She towel-dried her hair and dressed quickly. Another thought hit her while she brushed her teeth. There were some rivalries among members of the city council, but none that had turned bitter or even mildly sour. Still, debates did occur during council meetings.

If there was a bitter rivalry, finding a motive for the attack would be easier. At the same time, if the entire council always voted the same without the slightest amount of disagreement, it might be easier to pinpoint someone who had an issue with the entire city council. Instead, it seemed to Maggie that a healthy difference of opinion existed among the council members and the mayor. None of their disagreements seemed to rise to the level of an attack on the elected officials in the small town.

The question was, why would such a thing happen?

"Good morning," Brett said to her when she opened the bathroom door. He waited outside in the hall with a fresh cup of coffee for her.

"Thank you." Maggie smiled. She accepted the coffee and took a sip.

Brett's face fell. "Your eyes are bright red," he said. "Have you been crying?"

Maggie nodded slowly. "Yes, in bed before I got into the shower," she said. "It hit me again after I went back to bed that Ruby is in dire condition. And I just don't understand why the mayor was killed and the council members were poisoned."

Brett nodded. "None of us understand yet," he said. "To be completely honest with you, I don't have a clue about the reasons. We are looking through photos and videos of the ribbon cutting and that will lead us to a suspect, we hope. But there is nothing that indicates why this happened. There just isn't anything there."

"We probably won't know until we find the culprit," Maggie said.

"You're saying we quite a bit. Do you have a mouse in your pocket?"

Maggie smiled for the first time. "I can't help it."

Twenty minutes later, Brett headed out the back door. He paused before he left and leaned in for a final kiss. "Please let me know if anything changes while you're in Joplin," he said.

"I never said I was going back to the hospital," Maggie said, although that was her plan just as soon as she got her car from Orson, which Naomi had offered to help her with.

Brett smiled. "As if wild horses could keep you away." He left with a quick wave and headed to work.

CHAPTER SEVEN

Maggie called Bradley on the drive to Joplin, just to check in on things.

"Naomi said you were headed back to the hospital," he said before even saying hello.

"I am," Maggie said. "I really appreciate Zeke helping out in Dogwood Mountain."

"Can you let me know when you leave? I want to make sure you're alright, Mom."

"I will," she said. "I don't know how long I'll be there, but I'll keep in touch."

"Thanks," Bradley said. "This is off the subject, but I wanted to let you know that we offered those new gingerbread baked donuts you created."

"Did you? How'd it go?"

"Sold out in one hour." Bradley laughed. "We had to whip up two more batches just to make it through the morning."

Maggie chuckled lightly. "That's really great to hear," she said. "Just wait until I tell Ruby." Her voice faded.

Bradley sighed. "You'll get to tell her soon, Mom," he said. "I am absolutely sure of it. Maybe you'll be laughing about it with her by lunch."

"I hope you're right, Son," she said.

Maggie pushed the button on her steering wheel and ended the phone call. She blinked back the tears and concentrated on the road ahead of her. She turned up the music on the radio and sang along with the old country tunes all the way to the hospital exit.

Like most large towns, Joplin buzzed with traffic and people first thing in the morning. Maggie navigated through the traffic circle in front of the hospital. She made her way through the parking lot and chose a parking space close to one of the lights, just as Orson had done the day before. She had no idea how long she might be there.

She headed straight into the front entrance and waved to the women behind the registration desk as she passed them on her way to the elevators. She emerged from the elevator and walked toward the intensive care area. Right before she reached the waiting room, Maggie veered toward the nurses' station. She waited while the four nurses behind the desk continued their conversations. She didn't recognize any of them but was sad not to see Tanesha, the amazing nurse who had helped her before.

"Can I help you with something?" one of the nurses turned to ask.

"I'm here for Ruby Cobb," Maggie began. "She was brought here yesterday."

"Okay," the nurse said. Maggie searched for her name tag, but the badge was turned around. "What can I do for you?"

"Ruby is my, I mean, I'm Maggie Sharpe," she stumbled around for the right words. "I'm not her next of kin because we aren't related, but I am her emergency contact." She inhaled deeply. "I want to know how Ruby is doing. Is she any better? Can I go in and see her?"

"Maggie Sharpe, you said?" The nurse moved some things around on the desk. "Give me just a moment."

Maggie nodded. "Yes. I spoke with another nurse yesterday. Her name was Tanesha and she told me

Ruby has botulism and might have to go on a ventilator." She hoped the little bit of information would help things along. She also decided to leave out the fact that Brett had told her Ruby was already on a ventilator.

"Okay," the nurse said. Her voice and her features softened. "Let me check her chart and I'll get back to you. Go on and have a seat in the waiting room and I'll come and get you when I find out."

Maggie felt her spirits fall, sure the nurse would not actually come out and tell her anything. She pushed through the waiting room door and took a seat in the middle of the room. An elderly couple was seated on the far side of the room where she had sat with Orson the day before.

As soon as she took her seat, Maggie pulled her tablet out of her bag and powered it on. She waited while the hospital's internet matched with it and began scrolling through local news stories for information about the attack in Dogwood Mountain West. There was a small blurb in the local newspaper, local to Joplin, but that was all she could find.

"Ms. Sharpe?" Maggie looked up at the nurse standing in the waiting room doorway. She was not the same nurse she had spoken to before.

"I am," she said and lifted her arm in wave.

"I'm Tracy, and if you'll follow me, I have some information about your friend," she said. Maggie stood and immediately pushed her tablet back in her bag. She shouldered the bag and followed the nurse out into the hallway.

"Can you tell me what's going on?" Maggie asked as soon as they were free of the waiting room.

Tracy nodded. "I'll take you back to see Ruby in a few minutes, but I wanted to speak with you first," she said.

"Right," Maggie said, unsure what else to say.

"Okay, so there is no real change in her condition," Tracy said. "We are still waiting on some test results that will hopefully offer us more information."

"I thought that it was confirmed that it was botulism," Maggie asked.

Tracy shook her head. "When we suspect botulism, we always treat the patient like it is," she said. "There is no time to lose. We have a short window of time to deal with it and so we do."

"Okay," Maggie said. A new wave of panic hit her. If it wasn't botulism, what on earth could it be and why was Brett so sure it was, if it wasn't?

"Ruby is still not awake, and she is on the vent," the nurse continued. "Until she wakes up, it's hard to know where we're at."

Maggie swallowed hard. "Will she recover?"

Tracy looked around the hall and lowered her voice. "It's very hard to say at this point. Given her age, I don't know how to predict that. A doctor would be able to answer your questions better than I can," she said.

"Can I talk to the doctor?"

"Maybe, but for right now, I'm all you've got." Tracy smiled. "The other concern we have is whether or not she develops sepsis, which is a possibility. But we are doing everything we can to monitor and prevent that."

Maggie blinked back the tears again. "Can I see her?"

"You can see her for a short time," Tracy said.

Maggie nodded her head. "Okay."

Ten minutes later, Maggie followed the nurse into a darkened hospital room. She held onto Ruby's hand and listened to the soft whir of the ventilator. Machines and monitors beeped all around them.

"Listen up, Ruby," she said. "I'm going to need you to hurry up and get over whatever this is so you can get back to work. We're all going to pitch in and help look after the farm for a few days, but you know we have no idea what we're doing out there. Your farm hand is doing his best to deal with all of us."

She gazed at Ruby's motionless body and pale face. "Please hurry up and get better," she said, unable to say more. The nurse touched her lightly on her shoulder and she stood up, squeezed Ruby's hand again, and followed the nurse back out of the intensive care unit.

"You know, there is a chance she recovers completely in a short amount of time," Tracy said. "Depending on how fast she was brought into the hospital, it's not out of the question for her to be up and walking around like normal in a week or two."

Maggie smiled at the glimmer of hope the information gave her. "As soon as we noticed her symptoms, we tried to get her help."

"That's good." Tracy smiled. "That is very good."

Maggie thanked her for her help when she retrieved her bag and her tablet where she had left them behind the nurses' station. She headed back down to the elevators and out into the parking lot where she unlocked her car and climbed in. As soon as she was settled inside, she pulled out her phone and texted Brett.

"No change," she wrote in her message. "The nurse said she isn't completely sure it's botulism."

"Did you get to see her?" he replied.

"Maybe for ten minutes. Not long enough," Maggie responded.

She set the phone on the seat next to her and sat for a long moment. The tears spilled out of her eyes and down her face again. This time, Maggie did not hold them back.

CHAPTER EIGHT

"You don't need to be here right now," Orson grumbled at her when she stopped by the donut shop two hours later. Maggie had no intention of staying, but she did want to check in. She looked up at the large sign in Myra's handwriting that had been tacked up next to the menu behind the counter. "No boxed lunches until further notice," the note read. Her heart sank a little, but she shook her head and forced the thoughts away.

"I came in to check on all of you," she said to a hovering Orson. "And to tell you that I got to see Ruby."

Hopeful faces gathered around her. Zeke was the exception. He maintained his place in front of the deep fryer, but his sober glance told Maggie he did not expect good news.

"How was she?" Myra asked. "Is she awake?"

Maggie smiled sadly and shook her head. "She is not awake yet, but I told her that we were all pulling for her, and that she needed to hurry up and get back to her farm animals because not one of us knows what we're doing."

"Speak for yourself," Orson grumbled. "Paul told me I was his best farm hand assistant yet." He looked around the small group and shrugged his shoulders. "I have a lot more life experience than any of you combined." He slammed the towel in his hand down on the prep table and sulked out of the kitchen.

"He won't admit it, but this has him torn up inside," Myra said when the swinging door closed behind him.

"Yeah, he's been especially spicy," Naomi said. "I think the only reason he hasn't lined us all up for a whooping yet is because Zeke is here to keep things going."

"He seems to respect that smoldering masculine energy," Myra whispered.

"I heard that," Zeke said from the deep fryer. "And you're welcome." He turned toward them with a wide smile.

"Listen, I think Ruby is going to make a full recovery," Maggie said with as much conviction as she could muster. "I called Paul and told him I'm going to run out to the farm to meet him and help make sure the animals are fed."

"Please let us know the second you hear anything," Myra said before heading back out front.

"I will," Maggie promised. She hugged both women and turned to Zeke. "Thank you for being here. You are a gem."

"Oh, he doesn't mind being here," Myra said. "He loves the fact that he is so close to Flo."

Flo ran The Diner, a lunch and dinner food truck parked out on the other side of the donut shop parking lot.

"If you think you're going to get a rise out of me, you're mistaken," Zeke said. "But I'm not denying a word you said." Zeke's admiration of the food truck owner was a poorly held secret among them.

Maggie left the kitchen and headed up front. She wanted to hug Orson once before she left, even if he responded like a porcupine with his sharp quills.

She stepped through the swinging door and immediately looked at the Old Timer's table, but he wasn't there. She turned her head around and found him in the corner on the far side of the dining space close to the restrooms in the same booth where she always sat on her breaks with Ruby. With a sigh, Maggie walked around the corner to him. She placed her arm over his shoulders and leaned in to plant a kiss on the top of his head. Neither of them said a word.

True to her word, Maggie headed out to the farm next. Paul hadn't arrived yet, so she used the spare key to the back door and let herself into the house. As soon as the familiar scent of Ruby's kitchen hit her, she fought off a fresh wave of sadness. The entire house smelled of vanilla and cumin, just as she would expect in the home of a chef. She inhaled deeply and grabbed the spare keys to Beulah, Ruby's infamous flatbed farm truck, off the key rack by the fridge.

Beulah belched and struggled to start before her engine turned over at last. Maggie drove toward the large barn where the grain and hay were stored and began the process of feeding the animals, just as she had seen Ruby do many times before. She had ridden along in the passenger seat while Ruby had done the farm chores, chatting about a new donut variety, or complaining about Orson or, more often, Brett.

Expertly, she opened the gates and shut them behind her and waited while the animals gathered for their food. Somehow, though Maggie did not pretend to understand how, Ruby managed to run the farm and appear at the donut shop long before the sun came up in the morning. She knew Paul helped out a lot and that Ruby was glad to have him, but she still didn't understand how Ruby did it all.

"If only you had a clone," Maggie mumbled when she got back in the truck after shutting the gate behind her. Maybe if Ruby had one, the clone could be the one in the hospital bed and Ruby could get back to her life.

Maggie pressed her foot down on the accelerator and headed back to the house. Her speed was a little aggressive. Dirt clods flew out front the back tires when she pulled out. She slowed herself down immediately. Ruts in the yard was not something she cared to have to explain to Ruby when she was finally home.

When she parked the truck, she returned the keys to the kitchen and locked the house up behind her. Before she could leave, though, she had to take her usual wooden seat around the fire where she sat at least once each week unless the roads were too icy in the wintertime to make it out to the farm.

Maggie smoothed her hand down the wide arm rest and stared into the nonexistent fire. She sat back in the Adirondack chair and gazed up at the sky. By now, she would be seated at the booth in the corner with her coffee and her mid-morning snack waiting for Ruby to join her. They would sit and discuss the donut shop or some other concern weighing on them.

The longer she sat, the more her mind began to wonder about the reasons she was there in the first place. She decided to get up and run to her car for her tablet. Might as well do some looking around while she waited for Paul.

CHAPTER NINE

Mayor Jason Savino had been voted into office twice, both times with a landslide over whatever opponent decided to run against him. In both cases, the campaign was amiable. In the first election, his opponent was a sitting council member. After the election was over with, the mayor appointed the councilman to serve as his second in command.

Nothing she found about the mayor's history spoke of any major conflict. Next, Maggie began to search through local newspaper articles, going back six months. She read anything that she could find about local council meetings. Lately, most of the meetings were consumed by the Dogwood Mountain West project. And as far as she could tell, aside from a few questions about where the ribbon cutting would take place, she could not find any sort of debate whatsoever.

Maggie continued to look further back. She found one debate over the placement of a stop sign in a residential neighborhood on the other side of town. One councilwoman argued that the stop sign wasn't needed. Another raised concerns over two car accidents that had taken place there in the past year, but there was no smoking gun, nothing at all to indicate anyone might be upset enough to harm or murder members of the local government.

She set her tablet to the side and picked up her phone to check her messages. She had hoped to find a direction to go in, but so far, nothing stood out. She had a message from Bradley, simply checking in with her. She replied back quickly, telling him where she was and reassuring him that she was okay. Next she checked in with Brett. She sent a similar text to him, but she added a question.

"Has the investigation turned up any leads?"

"Nothing at all," Brett replied almost immediately. "I put in a call to the state police for assistance."

Maggie shuddered. She knew how much Brett appreciated the state police, but he preferred to handle as much of the county business as he could with his own department. Asking for assistance meant that there really was no direction he had found.

Next, she searched for each of the other targeted council members by name. Alice Reynolds was a school teacher who had been retired from the district for more than fifteen years. Her social media profiles were filled with pictures of grandchildren and the quilts she sewed for the children's hospitals in St. Louis and Kansas City.

Paul Simpson appeared to be close to the same age as Alice, but he was still employed as a general contractor in the area. From the city council meeting minutes she read on the city's website, Maggie discovered Paul was an outspoken critic of several infrastructure issues during several meetings. Once in a while, it appeared that the discussions could become heated, until Paul's wisdom from his background in construction won over other members.

Lastly, Connor Tewes tended to be the voice of the younger generation. His outlook on new businesses sometimes ruffled feathers, especially Paul's, when he spoke of the environmental impact new buildings might have. But Connor and Paul appeared to have come to a mutual respect for the other's views. She found a comment in some of the meeting notes from Paul in which he praised the younger man for bringing the environmental concerns to his attention.

"There is nothing here," Maggie said to herself. "Nothing whatsoever."

Maggie set the tablet down. She stood up and walked in a circle around the chairs. It was easier to think out in the country. Ruby's farm was nestled between two hills, just as it should be in the heart of the Ozarks.

She walked toward the old barn across the driveway from Ruby's white farmhouse. The inside of the barn had been somewhat modernized, but the outside looked like something out of an old movie. Myra and Brooks had been married there. Her mind wandered to the subject of her own upcoming wedding. While they had not specifically named the venue for their nuptials, she assumed that she and Brett would tie the knot right there in the barn on Ruby's farm.

There was only one thing she was sure of. Ruby would be the one standing next to her as her maid of honor.

"Come on and get better, Ruby," Maggie mumbled. She sighed and hugged her middle. The wind had cooled the air down considerably and she was not wearing a jacket. It was time to head back into town, she assumed. If only Tracy, the nurse she spoke to at the hospital that morning, was right. Ruby would be back on her feet soon.

Maggie looked toward the gravel road as she walked back toward the house and her car. She could hear the low rumble of a large tractor heading through the farm. She looked in time to wave at the green combine as it passed. Somehow, she'd missed Paul being there already. He must have parked farther into the property and gotten to work early. He grinned and waved back.

She stopped for a second. An image popped into her head, the green van that narrowly missed hitting her car right after the attack in Dogwood Mountain West. The scene replayed in her head. She stopped at the four-way intersection, ready to turn left. A dark green minivan waited at the stop sign to her right. She had waited for the van to go. It had clearly been there before her. She beeped the horn, and the driver, concealed by dark tinting, raced through the intersection, turning in front of her. The driver had narrowly missed plowing into the front of Orson's car. Later she heard from Orson that the driver had raced down the road past the donut truck.

Was it possible that the minivan driver might have been involved in the mayor's murder and the attack on city council? But why would someone involved in something so dire race back toward the scene of the crime moments after it happened?

Then there was the older woman walking down the street away from the chaos. Maggie had slowed down and offered her a ride back home, but the woman had refused. She would almost describe the refusal as aggressive. The woman's identity was a mystery to her, though based on the woman's business-like dress, Maggie had assumed that she was part of the city delegation, though could not pinpoint which part.

Just like the minivan driver, nothing made the woman seem like a potential suspect, either. Surely there were dozens of others who fled the scene on foot.

When she made it back to the bonfire circle, Maggie picked up her tablet and headed straight for her car. She wanted to go somewhere, to do something that felt like she was working toward an answer to the mystery of what had happened to her best friend. Once she was behind the wheel of the car, Maggie drove with no inclination to where she was headed, but by the time she reached the city limits of Dogwood Mountain, she knew exactly where she wanted to go.

As small towns go, Dogwood Mountain was not the smallest in the area, but with a population of only a few thousand people it was difficult to go somewhere and not bump into someone she knew. She was less familiar with the area of town annexed as Dogwood Mountain West. Although the zip code, school district, and the city government remained the same, the small community had simply been a collection of neighborhoods outside of town. Only recently had the word "west" been added to the small post office that served the area.

Maggie drove through town and headed for Dogwood Mountain West. She had no idea what she was going to do when she got there, but it was the only place she knew to begin.

CHAPTER TEN

When she spotted the post office again, Maggie turned down Cypress Street and slowed down when she passed the area where she had seen the green minivan two days before. She drove slowly and wondered if improvements to the streets and sidewalks in this newly incorporated area would be in their future.

She tried not to make herself too conspicuous driving through the residential neighborhoods, but she did spend an extra moment or two when she made a turn or slowed at an intersection just to give the block another quick scan in her mirrors.

Many of the houses along the residential streets resembled the rest of Dogwood Mountain. Of course, without any code enforcement, some differences did exist. Maggie spotted a number of houses with unused cars, some without tires, parked permanently in the front or along the side. For some, the grass had probably not been mowed since the middle of June. Others had discarded appliances stacked outside of a garage door or along the side of a house.

Most of the homes were quaint and well-kept, however. After a half hour or so, Maggie drove through the last neighborhood she planned to search and moved to the outskirts of the area. The land surrounding the houses increased. She turned around at the end of the road she was on and headed back to the more populated area.

Her grand plan had turned up nothing. She saw nothing even close to resembling a dark green minivan. Her choices were limited. She could run around forever in the country neighborhoods surrounding town. Maybe she would see something. Maybe not.

She could drive through the same neighborhoods once again and look a little harder, but she didn't want to call too much attention to herself. She slowed to the end of the long road and decided to go another quarter of a mile back around the edge of town. She turned onto a two lane county highway where houses lined one side of the road with pasture on the other side.

The road bent around a sharp turn and down a hill. Maggie spotted the entrance to a large trailer park. She slowed down and turned in. Driving through one more neighborhood couldn't hurt even though it was unlikely she'd find anything. At least in this area, the homes were much closer together than in any place she had found so far.

She moved along the first row of trailers, driving down the road until it circled back around to the opposite entrance. Four more roads intersected the rest of the park. Maggie turned around at the north entrance and followed the first interior road, pausing for each speed bump which she swore had been placed every twenty feet or so. By the end of the first road, she had seen every vehicle parked beside each of the single wide mobile homes up close and personal.

Maggie spotted the dark green minivan as she rounded the bend to the next road. It was parked halfway down the line of trailers to her right. She grabbed her phone off of the seat next to her and opened her camera. She pulled around the bend at the end of the road, then turned around in one of the driveways, heading back down the same street.

The good news was that there was another speed bump in front of the trailer where the minivan sat.

The bad news was the three scraggly-looking young men who stepped out on the small front porch when Maggie started back down the road. She slowed down to about ten miles per hour and positioned her phone on her lap. One of the men glanced down the road at her. She paused for the first speed bump, then released the steering wheel while she readied the camera in her hand.

Her plan was to snap a photo of the van when she drove over the speed bump in front of the driveway, but with the men out on the porch, she couldn't take a close up photo. Forced to think quickly, Maggie held the phone up in front of her face and smiled with pursed lips, like many of the younger women she had seen around town. She pretended to snap a selfie as she neared the van, and then another one as she pulled up closer.

Two of the men on the deck shouted a couple of strong words in her direction, then pretended to take photos of themselves as she passed. Maggie reacted by waving and speeding up as she drove back down the road toward the entrance. When she made it to the end of the road, she closed her window and rolled her eyes at her own behavior. Not only was she far too old to join anything trending among twenty-some-things but taking such photos of her own face was not in her nature.

Back out on the county highway, Maggie decided to turn the opposite way. She did not wish to drive through Dogwood Mountain West again, both from fear of being seen spending too much time driving around neighborhoods and from her own self-consciousness.

After twenty or so minutes, she spotted a turn off in front of a large field of winter wheat. She parked her car and checked her phone. The first photo turned out grainy and blurry. It was possible to make out the basic shape and the color of the minivan, but not much else. She struck gold with the second photo. Not only did she snap a clear view of the rear and the side of the minivan, but she also got a clear shot of the license plate and a view of the men on the deck. Their faces weren't perfectly clear, but she hoped the photo revealed enough about them that Brett could pull a decent description from it.

She called him immediately.

"What's wrong, Maggie?" he asked the second he answered the phone.

"Nothing," Maggie said. "Something may actually be right for a change."

"What are you talking about?" Brett asked. She

wasn't sure if he was irritated with her, or simply distracted and overwhelmed by the ongoing investigation into the mayor's death.

"I remembered something that happened when I was leaving after the ribbon cutting," she said, upset with herself for being so distracted. "A dark green minivan nearly hit the front end of Orson's car when I was driving back home. The driver of the van was hard to see because the windows were so darkly tinted. Anyway, the van raced through the intersection around me and sped down the road in front of Orson in the food truck."

"You didn't mention this to me earlier," Brett said.

"I honestly didn't think about it," Maggie said. "I was so consumed with worry about Ruby."

"What is your good news? That you remembered?"

"No," Maggie said patiently. "The good news is that I went back to Dogwood Mountain West to look for the van, and I found it."

"I have asked you not to throw yourself into the investigation," Brett said. "I have more to worry about than thinking my bride-to-be might be putting herself in danger."

"Brett, listen to me," Maggie said. "I am not in

danger. I simply drove around looking for the van. That's all. And I found it."

He sighed. "Where?"

"Do you know that large mobile home park that sits on the outskirts of town, to the west?"

"I do know, and if you were there, you most certainly were in danger," he said.

"Okay, well," Maggie said. "I found the van there. It's sitting in front of a trailer in the middle of the park. I got a picture of the van and the three men who were hanging around there."

"Wait, they saw you? I thought you said you had not put yourself into danger!" He raised his voice at her.

"Those men thought some middle-aged woman had slowed down over a speed bump to take a selfie with her phone. They had no idea I actually took one of them." She paused to send the photo to his cell phone.

"Okay," Brett said. "I just got the picture."

"Can you use that?" Maggie asked.

"Yeah," Brett said with a chuckle. "We can definitely use this. You even managed to get the address on the trailer in the photo."

"I did?" Maggie asked, surprised. She hadn't

looked too closely at the trailer behind the van in the photo.

"You got three amazing pieces of evidence in a single photo, and you didn't even know it," Brett said.

"Maybe my next stop should be the police academy," she joked.

"Hilarious."

Maggie could almost hear his eyes rolling in his head.

CHAPTER ELEVEN

Instead of going back home, Maggie returned to Ruby's farm after she spoke with Brett about the green minivan. She walked straight to the Adirondack chairs and took a seat, breathing a sigh of relief. Images of Brett walking one of the men from the trailer away in handcuffs filled her head. Maybe she had helped find the person who hurt her best friend and murdered the mayor. Maybe Ruby would wake up soon and tell Brett what she saw. The responsible person would be on his way to prison and their lives could go on.

Life would have to go on. Maggie thought about the donut shop for the first time in a while. What would it be like if Ruby was in the hospital for a long time? It was possible she would not even want to return after this scare. Maybe retirement would be a new chapter in her life. For that matter, maybe the upcoming chapter in her own life would mean less time at the donut shop. She could hire a couple of part-time helpers and promote Naomi. For Pete's sake, she was more than capable.

Then, if Ruby decided not to return to the donut shop kitchen, Maggie herself could work fewer hours and spend more time with Brett at home and Ruby wherever adventure took them. She smiled at the thought.

For now, the donut shop was still her full time job, and then some. She picked up her phone and called Myra to check in on things.

"Maggie," she said breathlessly. "Is there anything new about Ruby?"

Maggie sighed. "No," she said. "I wish I could report something new, or at least something good."

"Maybe soon," Myra said.

"Definitely soon," Maggie replied. "I just wanted to check in with you and see how things are going there? Are you all making it?"

"We're doing great," Myra said. "Zeke does the job of two people, and without the lunch boxes, we are able to close earlier."

"Are you saying you don't want the lunch boxes

to return?" Maggie regretted the question and her tone the second it came out of her mouth.

"No, no, I didn't mean that," Myra said. "I just mean that we're not as busy. I want the lunch boxes back. I never want them to go away."

Maggie exhaled slowly. Just like her, Myra was not talking about the lunch boxes. "I think I know what you meant," she said. "Please don't take anything from what I said. I'm just tired."

"I think you're more than just tired," Myra said. "You sound emotionally exhausted."

"I think I am," Maggie said. She ended the phone call with Myra and closed her eyes. She shivered slightly in the chilly wind. The temperature had dropped, and the wind had picked up. A stray raindrop hit her face, but Maggie had no desire to move from where she was sitting. She might remain right where she was seated until Ruby came home.

Somewhere between her phone call with Myra and her thoughts about Ruby, Maggie fell asleep in her chair. Her phone rang and jolted her awake an hour later. She answered without checking the screen.

"Hello!"

"Maggie? Are you okay?" Brett asked her.

"Yeah, I'm fine." Maggie pushed herself up higher on her seat. "I'm just at Ruby's."

"What are you doing out there?" he asked her.

"I don't know," Maggie admitted. "It just felt like the place to go."

"Are you sure you're okay?" he asked.

"I would be better if you called to tell me that you made an arrest," Maggie said.

"I wish I could tell you that," he said.

Maggie felt her spirit fall even lower. "So, the green minivan?"

"Turned out to be a dead-end," he said. "We ran the plates and showed up at the trailer park."

"What happened?"

"The guys you saw were in it and up to no good," he said. "When we paid them a visit they were all flying high as kites in March. But they sobered up real fast when I told them I wanted to question them about the murder of the mayor of Dogwood Mountain."

"You don't think they were involved?"

"Not in the least," he said. "First, I don't think they have enough brain cells left between them to put together something like a murder of a local official and a getaway plot. And secondly, they were driving around in a dispute that day, and one of my deputies pulled them over and gave them all tickets for no seat belts. The van was searched for drugs or paraphernalia. There was no evidence that they were involved in the death of the mayor or the poisoning of the others."

"Are you completely sure?"

"I am very sure," he said. "I want nothing more than to find who is responsible for this."

The tears returned to her eyes. "I wish that had turned into something," she said. "I almost wish the older lady I tried to give a ride to after that would have gotten into the car with me. If I knew who she was, maybe I could find out if she has some information that would lead us to who did this."

"What are you talking about?" Brett asked her. "What woman?"

"I told you about her," Maggie said. "She was walking away from the ribbon cutting in a hurry and she was in heels, no less. I was just trying to be nice to her."

"I don't recall you telling me about this woman," Brett said gently. "Do you know who she was?"

"I have no idea," Maggie said, second guessing if she'd mentioned it to him at all. Maybe the police academy wasn't actually in her future.

"Can you come down to my office? There are some photos I want you to look at."

"I'm on my way."

CHAPTER TWELVE

"That's her,' Maggie said. She was seated in the leather chair behind Brett's desk at the sheriff's department.

"Are you sure?" Brett asked her.

"Positive," Maggie said. She looked up at him. "Who is she? I think I've seen her at a council meeting once or twice before, but I just thought she served on a committee or something."

"Her name is Ethel Groves and she's a local business owner," Brett said. "She runs an herbal shop just outside of town."

"Is she a suspect?" Maggie asked.

"I don't see how," Brett said. "But I'm going to take a ride out to her shop. I know just where it is."

"Okay, well, let me know what happens."

"What are you going to do?" Brett asked her, a look of worry coming over his face.

"Go home, I guess," she said. It wasn't something that she had admitted to herself, but she had been avoiding the prospect of returning to her empty house only to sit there alone with her thoughts.

"I'll call you as soon as there's anything to call about," Brett said. He leaned over and kissed her on the top of her head. "I expect you to do the same if you hear anything from the hospital."

"Part of me wants to go back to Joplin and sit there with her until she wakes up," Maggie said. "But I don't even know if they would let me see her again."

"It might be a waste of time," Brett said. "I know that sounds terrible, but it could be better just to wait it out at home."

Maggie followed him back out into the parking lot. She headed to Dogwood Mountain rather than going toward Joplin and the hospital. She fought everything in her to turn around and follow Brett to meet this Ethel woman. Something about the look in her eyes from the photos haunted her.

Surely, she told herself, she was imagining it all. She had a vague memory of the woman on the day the mayor was killed, but it felt like a lifetime ago. But there was something that nagged hard at her as she drove through town. She pulled into the grocery store parking lot and parked on the edge, away from the other cars. She was less than two miles from home, but her instincts told her not to wait.

Maggie reached over and pulled out her tablet. Her battery was good, and the cellular signal was strong. She opened the search engine and typed in "Ethel Groves." At first, nothing stood out to her. She found seven obituaries for women by the same name scattered across the middle south, mostly in Arkansas.

"No, there's something here," she said to herself. "I just know it." She cleared the search box and added "Ethel Groves, Herbalist" next.

Immediately the page populated. Ethel had a large online presence, though Maggie didn't recognize many of the websites she was listed on. She found her name mentioned in numerous blogs, though most of them were a little vague.

Maggie picked the first blog and clicked on it. She looked for a more specific description of the site. All she found was, "If you're here, you know why." Her only choice was to click on posts and begin reading.

As she dug deeper, it was clear she had stumbled upon the blog of an environmental activist. Most of the recent blog entries focused on the deforestation in rural areas, mostly because of agricultural efforts and tourism.

"Our mission is to stop the pillage of nature, as much as there is left to save. And while the Ozarks are not the most deforested area in the United States, there is still much work to be done."

Reading a little further, she spotted Ethel's name among the activist-friendly business owners in the area, but nothing more. Maggie clicked out of the blog and scrolled down further on the page. She picked randomly and clicked on another blog title. Immediately, the posts caught her eye. "By Whatever Means Necessary" was the name of the blog, though in the search engine it was listed simply as "The Environmentally Concerned." Ethel's name was prominent in the comments.

"Everyone is so concerned over deforestation in rural areas," Ethel wrote, according to the name on the website. "Why doesn't anyone ever consider the damage done to the water supply when small towns expand?"

Maggie felt her heart race. She sat up higher in her seat and began to scan the rest of the comments on the page. The discussion thread under Ethel's comment went on for three pages.

"What do you suggest we do about it?" another commenter asked toward the end of the thread.

"It isn't like we can do anything to stop City Hall," another wrote.

Ethel's reply was stark and simple. The words seemed to stare back at her from the tablet screen. "Wanna bet?"

"Oh, no," Maggie breathed out the words. "Brett is walking into something bad." She set the tablet on the passenger seat and picked up her phone. She searched for the address of the herbal shop and headed that way.

Not long after, she was parked outside a metal building with a corrugated steel roof. She tried calling Brett, but he failed to answer. By the looks of the parking lot, he was likely the only one inside. Maggie felt panic rising up inside of her. She shook it off and called Brooks.

"Hey, Maggie," he said when he answered. "Is there any word on Ruby?"

"No, no," Maggie said. "Listen, Brett is out here in the new annexed area at an herbal shop owned by Ethel Groves."

"I know the place," Brooks said.

"I don't know if he told you, but I saw her walking away from the ribbon cutting the other day.

She was dressed up like she was going to church and walking away very quickly," Maggie explained as fast as the words could leave her mouth. "Brett had me look over some photos and we identified her. Brooks, I searched for her on the internet. I think she might have something to do with what happened."

"What did Brett say?" he asked.

"I haven't told him about what I found yet," Maggie said.

"Where are you?"

"At the herbal shop. Brett's inside and I'm in my car."

"Whatever you do, stay outside," Brooks said. "I'll be there in less than three minutes."

Maggie ended the phone call and gripped the steering wheel. She considered ignoring his instructions and going inside anyway. After all, what if Brett was in trouble? As soon as she placed her hand on the door handle, her phone rang again. She didn't recognize the number but answered it quickly.

"Hello?"

"Is this Ms. Sharpe? Maggie Sharpe?"

"It is."

"Maggie, we met earlier," the woman continued. "This is Tracy Ortiz from Mercy Hospital in Joplin."

"Oh, goodness," Maggie said. She pinched the

bridge of her nose. "I remember you. Is everything okay?"

"Well, I'm calling because I have some very good news," she said. "Ruby's doctors are with her right now, and she was taken off the vent. She's weak, but she's going to be okay."

"Are you sure?" Maggie asked. "You're sure she is going to be okay?"

"Positive," Tracy said. Maggie could hear the smile in her voice. "With botulism, and in her specific case, patients make a full recovery if they seek medical help immediately."

"I can't tell you how happy that makes me right now," Maggie said, glad they knew exactly what poisoned Ruby. That was hopefully one step closer to figuring out who was responsible and why. "Should I come up there? Can I come and see her?"

"I'd give her until the morning," Tracy said. "Chances are, she's going to have to meet with occupational therapy and respiratory care before the end of the day. It will probably wear her out, and the more rest she gets, the sooner she will be able to go home."

As she ended the phone call with Tracy, Maggie could hear the wail of sirens in the distance. Brooks was coming, and it sounded like the cavalry was coming with him.

CHAPTER THIRTEEN

"What is it with you and your instincts?" Brett was seated on the tailgate of an ambulance. His eyes were red from the solution the paramedic had poured in them. Maggie turned from him only long enough to watch Ethel Groves walk past in handcuffs.

"Shame on you, Sheriff," the old woman called as she passed. Two officers dressed in hazmat suits escorted her to another waiting ambulance.

"Have fun in prison," Brett muttered under his breath. "I wish I could pour some of whatever this is over her head and see how she likes it."

"Lucky for you it was just a light concentration of stinging nettle," the paramedic said behind him. "I did, however, hear the fire department say it's going to take an actual hazardous materials team to come in here and clean this all up."

"How does one brew botulism anyway?" Brett asked. "I'm not making light of it or anything. But how do you do that?"

"What I want to know is how someone can slip a toxin into the drinking water of four city council members and manage to stab the mayor in the back with a pair of scissors without being seen," Brooks said.

"She was seen alright, just not by anybody that was looking," Brett said.

"I don't know what you mean," Maggie admitted.

"Think about it," Brett said. He dabbed his skin with the soaked towel the paramedic had given him. "She was barely visible to anyone who was around her. She neither looks nor acts like an activist or anyone who might want to cause trouble. It was only online that she let her true colors be known."

"Until she plotted an attack on the city," Maggie said. "And even then she was able to slip in and out practically invisible."

"That's because she was invisible," Brett said. "Everyone around here thinks of her as an odd but harmless older woman who runs the herb shop.

Nobody knew we had much more of a disaster right under our noses."

"But why? What was her issue with the mayor and the city council annexing a few hundred houses? I don't get it," Brooks said.

"She said something about saving the water table from the humans before she threw that bottle of stuff all over me," Brett said. "She admitted to poisoning the water of the city council members, but she said the plan to kill the mayor didn't hit her until she watched him cut the ribbon with those ceremonial scissors."

"Then why did she do it?" Brooks asked.

"Because the opportunity presented itself." Brett shrugged. "And when she spotted the backup pair of scissors on the podium for the ribbon cutting, she decided the best way to stop other small town mayors from doing the same thing was to kill Jason Savino. She counted on it, creating a fear factor."

"By whatever means necessary," Maggie repeated. "That was what she said online."

Brett shook his head. "Who knows what would have happened if you hadn't been so diligent and followed your gut." He leaned over and tried to kiss her. "Will you be my wife?"

"I already told you yes," Maggie said, wiping the mess off of her cheek. "But get out of here. You smell like a rotten daisy."

CHAPTER FOURTEEN

Maggie tied her apron behind her back with a flourish. She smoothed the front down over her clothes and turned to the baker's table. The decision to close the donut shop on a Sunday morning shocked the members of her staff, most especially Orson who asked her three times if she had somehow lost her mind from the stress of the past few days. Maggie assured him that she felt more in charge of her own mind than she had in the past week and that the news of Ruby's recovery had certainly helped out a lot. The fact that she was home and able to leave the house was good enough reason to close as far as Maggie was concerned.

She picked up the large stainless steel mixing bowl and began measuring cake flour into it. One at a time, Maggie measured out the dry ingredients and stirred them into the flour, then added dark cocoa powder last of all. The dusty brown color of the mixture brought a smile to her face. She stirred in melted butter, cooled slightly, and the eggs then mixed in the milk.

While the small batch of donuts baked, she turned to the double boiler on top of the stove to make the ganache for the top. She had promised Ruby a simple brownie donut while she was in the hospital, but the simplicity of the recipe belied the excitement she felt preparing a treat for the members of her family. Bradley promised to arrive by nine with Wyatt and Jake in tow. Zeke and Flo were coming, curiously together. Brooks, Myra, Orson, and Lexi were due any time as well. Naomi and Josie had arrived five minutes after Maggie, and they'd prepared large batches of coffee while Maggie finished the donuts. They also worked on two large breakfast casseroles which were now cooling on the prep table while the donuts baked.

While she waited, Maggie opened the walk-in cooler and brought out two large bowls of cut fruit she had prepared at home. She carried the bowls out to the counter and set them down. Naomi carried two chairs toward the center of the dining area where she had already pushed together four tables and set up a high chair for Lexi and a booster seat for Wyatt.

"Do you think we'll all fit?" she asked Maggie when she set the chairs down.

"We have before." Maggie smiled.

"And we're more than ready to do it again," Brooks said as he walked through the swinging door. He carried Lexi in his arms, followed by Myra and Orson, who brought up the rear with a scowl on his face.

"I never understood why babies require so much stuff," he said and set a large backpack down on the counter next to the bowls of fruit.

"I told you I'd carry that, Orson," Myra said.

"What and let the two of you do all the work?" Orson asked. "That's not the way this works."

Myra winked in Maggie's direction while the men sparred over the responsibilities of parents versus the adopted grandfather.

Bradley arrived with Jake and Wyatt behind him. Wyatt immediately took off running for Orson who had seated himself between Josie and Lexi. Without a break in his conversation, he picked up Maggie's grandson and placed him on his lap. Zeke and Flo came next. As promised, she brought a large platter of homemade biscuits and a tureen of sausage gravy with her.

"I'll be right back," Maggie announced. She glanced at the clock. The donuts had cooled long enough for her to pipe on the ganache and top them with the multi-colored candies Wyatt loved so much. She stood over the baker's table and iced two trays of the donuts. It was clear that she had made way more than she needed to for their gathering, but the abundance felt good.

The back door opened, and Brett stepped inside. She froze with the icing bag in her hand. He was arm in arm with Ruby as they walked slowly into the kitchen. Maggie noticed how she also used her hand along the door and then the walls to help balance herself.

"Ruby." Maggie set the piping bag down on the table and walked slowly around the side. She felt the tears sting her eyes.

"I understand we have you to thank for cracking the case," Ruby said, her voice hoarse.

"I think Brett had more to do with it this time," Maggie said. She hesitated, then wrapped her arms carefully around her best friend.

"I'm not going to break," Ruby said. "My doctors

told me that I must be a tough old bird to come out of this relatively unscathed."

"I really can't believe that you don't have any lasting damage from all of this," Maggie said.

"You do know why, don't you?" Ruby asked. "It's only because you and Orson acted so quickly to get me the help that I needed that I came out so much better." She shuffled slowly toward the middle of the kitchen. "What's going on over here? Is this a new donut?"

"Are you really that shocked?" Brett teased. "I swear once we get hitched, I'll be the butt of jokes at work from all of the weight I'm going to gain."

Maggie and Ruby turned to glare at him at the same time. "What are you trying to say here, Sheriff?" Ruby asked him.

"Are you making a statement about the weight of people who already eat my cooking, Sheriff?" Maggie added.

"Help," Brett said quietly at first, then raised his voice. "Help! Somebody help me!"

Brooks burst through the kitchen door first. "What's going on, man?" he asked. He was joined quickly by Naomi and Bradley.

"Did something happen?" Naomi asked.

"He just got himself into hot water back here is

all," Ruby said. Her voice sounded slightly stronger than a moment before.

"Why don't we all just sit down and have breakfast before anyone else gets into trouble?" Brooks suggested.

Maggie grabbed the first tray of brownie donuts and Naomi took the other tray. They dropped them off on the small bit of counter space that was left and joined everyone else at the table.

"Before we have breakfast," Orson stood up to say. "I just want to take a moment to thank Maggie."

"What are you thanking me for?" Maggie asked, a little surprised.

"Well, if it wasn't for you taking over this place after your aunt died, I never would have met the rest of you and I wouldn't have spent the last week losing sleep over whether one of you was going to live or not," he said.

"Orson," Myra whispered. "What are you doing?"

Orson held up both hands. "Just let me finish," he said. "The truth of the matter is, until all of you came into my life, I had only one person to concern myself with. It was an easier existence at times, fewer people in your life means less heartache."

Maggie felt her stomach churn as he spoke. She moved her feet around under her chair, ready to run to the bathroom rather than break down crying in front of everyone.

"But a single life is also a quiet one, without the chaos of love and friendship. You have to know the lows in order to feel the highs," he said. "While my heart has been breaking over the past week, I wouldn't miss this for all of the quiet space in the world. So, thank you, Maggie, for bringing this crazy quilt of people together."

Maggie didn't try to blink back the tears. She stood up from her chair and walked around behind Orson, wrapping her arms unapologetically around him. One by one they each rose and hugged him in turn. When Brett approached him, he stopped and placed one hand on his shoulder.

"I actually have something I want to say," he said. "You all know that we're going to celebrate a special event in a few months."

Bradley began humming The Wedding March. Maggie wadded a napkin up and tossed it at him.

"I know that it's typically the bride who brings an entourage with her to the altar, but I decided not to be outdone," Brett said. "Orson, I've already asked Brooks to be one of my groomsmen at the wedding. I planned to ask Bradley as well, but he has another job to do first."

"I do? What's that?" Bradley asked.

"I think you're going to walk your mom down the aisle," Ruby whispered.

"Ah." Bradley nodded. He picked up the napkin and tossed it back at his mother. "I guess she did already ask me that."

Brett turned back to Orson. "That leaves the job of best man," he said. "What do you say?"

"Are you asking me to be your best man, Sheriff?" Orson said in a husky voice.

Brett nodded. "As long as you aren't busy that day," he said.

"Can I get a pass on my next speeding ticket?" Orson asked, grinning.

"I think we can work something out," Brett said.

"In that case, I'd be honored," Orson said.

Maggie clapped her hands together in delight. Brett and Orson embraced for a moment. When he took his seat again, Maggie noted the tears rolling down his wrinkled cheeks.

AUTHOR'S NOTE

I'd love to hear your thoughts on my books, the storylines, and anything else that you'd like to comment on—reader feedback is very important to me. My contact information, along with some other helpful links, is listed on the next page. If you'd like to be on my list of "folks to contact" with updates, release and sales notifications, etc.… just shoot me an email and let me know. Thanks for reading!

Also…

… if you're looking for more great reads, Summer Prescott Books publishes several popular series by outstanding Cozy Mystery authors.

CONTACT SUMMER PRESCOTT BOOKS PUBLISHING

Blog and Book Catalog: http://summerprescottbooks.com

Email: summer.prescott.cozies@gmail.com

And…be sure to check out the Summer Prescott Cozy Mysteries fan page and Summer Prescott Books Publishing Page on Facebook – let's be friends!

To sign up for our fun and exciting newsletter, which will give you opportunities to win prizes and swag, enter contests, and be the first to know about New Releases, click here: http://summerprescottbooks.com

Made in the USA
Columbia, SC
15 March 2023

13816217R00065